RANDOM HARRY POTTER FACTS YOU DON'T KNOW

(154 Fun Facts and Secret Trivia)

by: Mariah Caitlyn

Edited by Tom F. Whitehall (b02)

V2A

1. The Death Eaters were once called The Knights of Walpurgis.

2. Dragon liver costs 16 sickles per ounce. They originally cost 17 sickles per ounce in an early book but their price was later retconned because 17 sickles is equal to one galleon.

3. There are 142 staircases at Hogwarts.

4. After Steven Spielberg decided not to direct the first movie, he recommended M. Night Shyamalan for the project but he also turned it down.

5. Fred and George Weasley were born on April 1st, also known as April Fool's Day.

6. Natalie McDonald, a first-year student in *Goblet of Fire* was named after a real girl who died of leukemia. She wrote to JK Rowling asking her what would happen in the series because she wouldn't live to see it, but by the time JK Rowling replied, Natalie had died.

7. Mrs. Figg's job title was Kneazle Breeder.

8. Ginny Weasley became a professional Quidditch player and played for the Holyhead Harpies. She retired early to take care of her children.

9. Minerva once fell in love with a Muggle.

10. Both Professor McGonagall and Professor Flitwick were Hatstalls between Gryffindor and Ravenclaw. A Hatstall is someone who takes more than five minutes to be sorted into a house.

11. "Expecto patronum" is Latin for "I expect protection."

12. In the early days of Quidditch, seekers chased a small golden bird called a snidget. But they were going extinct so golden snitch was created.

13. The entire series is told from the point of view of only four characters. Harry Potter, Vernon Dursley, Frank Bryce and the Prime Minister of the United Kingdom.

14. Hermione, Ron, and Harry were all immortalized on Chocolate Frog cards.

15. Tonks's Patronus started out as a jack rabbit and later changed to wolf.

16. Ron's Patronal form was a Jack Russell Terrier while Hermione's was an otter. Jack Russell Terriers are known to chase otters.

17. Dumbledore means "Bumblebee" in old English.

18. The owls used in the Harry Potter movies are all from Massachusetts, USA.

19. Michael Gambon, the actor who replaced Richard Harris as Dumbledore, has never read a single Harry Potter book.

20. In the second movie, fourteen cars were destroyed to create the scene where Harry and Ron crashed into the Whomping Willow.

21. 62442, the password to enter the Ministry as a visitor spells out 'magic' on a phone.

22. After Fred died, George was never again able to create a Patronus.

23. Mr. Dursley's company is called Grunnings.

24. The role of Hagrid was the first character to be cast in first movie.

25. Winky the house-elf never got
    past her addiction to Butterbeer.

26. Dumbledore's favorite flavor of
    jam is raspberry.

27. In the books, Hermione has buck
    teeth, but this was changed for
    the movies because Emma
    Watson couldn't speak properly
    with the prosthetic teeth.

28. Emma Watson was the last girl in her school to audition for the role of Hermione Granger. She didn't even to want to do it at first, but her teacher convinced her.

29. Total running time for all 8 movies is 18 hours and 57 minutes.

30. Harry Potter does not successfully cast a single spell in the first movie. What a great wizard!

31. The set director intentionally bought the ugliest furniture she could find in order to make the Dursley's house seem as uncomfortable as possible.

32. In the movies, the child actors were doing real homework to make the scene more realistic.

33. George and Fred threw snowballs at Voldemort.

34. The actor who played Lucius Malfoy didn't want to act in *Deathly Hallows* because his character had been imprisoned at end of *Order of the Phoenix.* JK Rowling informed him his character was released in an early scene and he signed back on to the project.

35. In the movies, Dobby's puppet is just a ball on a stick. The rest of him is added in digitally.

36. 211,150 fake coins were made for the Gringotts vault set.

37. Daniel Radcliffe was paid £1 million for the film, making him the youngest actor ever (11-years-old) to be paid over a million dollars for a role.

38. JK Rowling said she killed Hedwig because it represented the loss of innocence and security. The owl's death marked the end of Harry's childhood.

39. Luna Lovegood became a naturalist after she graduated and then married Rolf Scamander. They had twin sons, Lorcan and Lysander.

40. Dementors are based off JK Rowling's years of depression in her twenties.

41. The Hogwarts school motto is "Never tickle a sleeping dragon."

42. Hagrid is 8 foot 6.

43. The tattoos on Sirius Black's body are modeled after Russian prison and street gangs.

44. The shortest book (*Chamber of Secrets*) was the longest movie.

45. In *Deathly Hallows: Part 1* the actress who played Luna Lovegood designed most of her clothing, jewelry, and the accoutrements found in the Lovegood home. She even choreographed her own dance moves for the wedding scene.

46. The longest book (*Order of the Phoenix)* was the shortest movie.

47. Alan Rickman was hand-picked to play Snape by JK Rowling. He was the only actor given secret information from JK Rowling about his character.

48. Hermione's last name was Puckle in early drafts of the first book.

49. The 12th use for dragon blood is as an oven cleaner.

50. *Chamber of Secrets* is Daniel Radcliffe's favorite book.

51. Snape protected Harry for two reasons. One, he was in love with Lily. Two, he had a life debt to James, who saved him from Lupin.

52. The Durmstrang Institute is in Sweden.

53. The last Harry Potter movie set the record for highest-grossing opening weekend, but it was broken less than a year later by *The Avengers.* That record was broken by *Jurassic World* and that record was broken by *Star Wars: The Force Awakens.*

54. The bats you see flying around Hagrid's hut in the movies are real. The trainers used bananas to control them.

55. The spell that opens Dumbledore's office is Sherbet Lemon

56. Moaning Myrtle was a member of Ravenclaw house.

57. Guillermo del Toro had the opportunity to direct the third Harry Potter movie but chose instead to do *Hellboy*.

58. Guillermo del Toro also turned down an opportunity to direct the sixth movie and chose instead to do *Hellboy 2: The Golden Army*.

59. Rosie O'Donnell and Robin Williams both wanted to be in the Harry Potter movies so badly they offered to work for no pay.

60. Chris Columbus was chosen to direct the first movie because of his experience with childhood actors. He was not JK Rowling's first choice. That was Terry Gilliam.

61. Lupin was the first werewolf to receive the Order of Merlin, First Class. It was awarded to him posthumously.

62. Voldemort was 71-years-old when he died at the Battle of Hogwarts.

63. *Harry Potter and the Half-Blood Prince* had the highest marketing budget but the lowest return on investment.

64. In total, 25,237 costumes and pieces of clothing were needed for the Harry Potter movies.

65. Vandals defaced the Hogwarts Express train and caused a three-day delay in shooting. They were never caught.

66. In the movie *Die Hard*, Alan Rickman is pushed off a building and falls to his death. In the sixth Harry Potter movie, a similar scene is shot but this time it is Alan Rickman pushing somebody else off a building.

67. Despite ending up married, Harry Potter and Ginny Weasley only kiss once during the movies.

68. The spell "Lumos" is also the name of JK Rowling's charity for children.

69. Warner Brother wanted to make Harry Potter an animated series and combine several books into one movie but JK Rowling said "Forget it."

70. *Chamber of Secrets* was the first movie to sell a million DVD copies in the first weekend in the UK.

71. Hugh Grant was originally going to play Gilderoy Lockhart but left the project abruptly without ever explaining why.

72. During the filming of the Harry Potter movies three accidental fires were started and one set burned to the ground and had to be rebuilt.

73. When she saw the set for Hermione's bedroom, Emma Watson told the set designers: "There should be more books." They made it so.

74. The third movie sold the least amount of tickets, VHS copies, DVDs, and made the least amount of money worldwide.

75. Dobby's flappy ears were based on a dog named Max that used to sit in the art department under a desk. He belonged to one of the designers.

76. Helen McCrory was originally cast as Bellatrix Lestrange, but due to an unexpected pregnancy she was replaced by Helena Bonham Carter.

77. The actor who plays Ron (Rupert Grint) is terrified of spiders. Whenever there is a scene in the movies with spiders, the horrified looks on his face are completely real.

78. Daniel Radcliffe went through more than 160 pairs of glasses while filming the Harry Potter movies.

79. The entire 19-years-later epilogue at the end of the movie series had to be reshot because of make-up issues.

80. M. Night Shyamalan turned down directing the third movie so he could direct *The Village.*

81. Gary Oldman gave Daniel Radcliffe a bass guitar when they first met on set. It was well-known that Daniel loved music.

82. Voldemort drank a bad love potion when he was young and was incapable of feeling love.

83. Harry arrived at Privet Drive for the first time with Hagrid on Sirius' motorcycle, and left Privet Drive for the last time with Hagrid on Sirius' motorcycle.

84. While filming an underwater scene for *Goblet of Fire*, Daniel Radcliffe accidently signaled he was drowning, and sent rescue teams into a panic. They dived into the pool and dragged him to the surface and started to perform CPR.

85. *Harry Potter and the Deathly Hallows* was originally supposed to be one movie, but the screenplay ended up being over 500 pages long. Most movie scripts are between 90 and 120 pages so it had to be made in two parts.

86. The radish earrings worn by Luna Lovegood were actually crafted by the actress herself, Evanna Lynch.

87. Cho Chang got married to a muggle.

88. A total of 13 ear infections were reported as a result of filming underwater scenes in the Harry Potter movies.

89. *Deathly Hallows: Part 1* was supposed to be released in 3D. The 3D version was cancelled at the last minute because it wasn't ready for the release date. The producers would have had to push back the release date by 3 months to make it work.

90. Over the course of the films there were two outbreaks of head lice amongst the younger cast.

91. The street that Harry and Hagrid walk down to get to the Leaky Cauldron is the same street Sean Connery waits for Catherine Zeta-Jones in the movie Entrapment.

92. Hermione is younger than both Harry and Ron, but Emma Watson is older than Daniel Radcliffe and Rupert Grint.

93. Michael Jackson wanted to do a Harry Potter musical but JK Rowling said "Forget it."

94. The Parseltongue language used in the movies was created by a professional linguist.

95. The reason paintings can talk and photos can't is because paintings are created by witches and wizards and they are able to cram more of the subject's personality into the art.

96. The Game Keeper before Hagrid was Ogg.

97. More than 3,000 girls auditioned for the role of Cho Chang, making it the largest audition for a secondary character in UK history.

98. On the final day of filming, Rupert Grint (Ron) gave Daniel Radcliffe and Emma Watson a trumpet. It was a strange gift and he never explained why.

99. In the fifth movie, during the breakfast scenes in the Great Hall, boxes of cereal can be seen with the names Cheeri-Owls and Pixie-Puffs. Both boxes have color schemes similar to those of Cheerios and Sugar Puffs.

100. Daniel Radcliffe's stunt-double was badly injured while filming the aerial sequence for *Deathly Hallows: Part 1.*

101. The acne problems that come with teen actors was solved with digital make-up. They tested real make-up but it looked terrible in close-up shots.

102. *Goblet of Fire* was originally written as two films, but the screenplays were merged and they became one film.

103. Hagrid is the only main character JK Rowling had planned to have survive the series.

104. The oldest actress to portray a Hogwarts student was Shirley Henderson (Moaning Myrtle) who was 37-years-old at the time of filming.

105. In the last film's epilogue, Draco Malfoy's wife was played by the actor's real life girlfriend, actress Jade Gordon.

106. *Prisoner of Azkaban* was the last Harry Potter movie to be released on VHS.

107. A special clause in Alfonso Cuarón's contract forbade the director from cursing in front of the kids actors.

108. For the fifth movie, Dumbledore's line "Don't fight him, Harry, you can't win," was featured in every trailer and TV spot, yet is nowhere in the final version of the film, nor in the DVD extended scenes or director's cut.

109. The Weasley twins were only apart twice. Once when George's ear was cursed off, and again when Fred was killed.

110. Emma Watson was "this close" to abandoning the Harry Potter movies due to personal issues after the fourth movie, but her parents convinced her to finish the series.

111. Dobby was written out of the fourth movie in favor of longer scenes for Neville Longbottom.

112. Despite denying it many times, JK Rowling has admitted (off the record) that some traits of Gilderoy Lockhart were based on her ex-husband.

113. JK Rowling changed the name of the fourth book from *Harry Potter and the Triwizard Tournament* to *Harry Potter and the Goblet of Fire* only a short time before submitting the original draft to her editor.

114. Ian McKellen turned down the role of Dumbledore because he didn't want to be both Gandalf *and* Dumbledore. Also, the actor

115. Katie Leung auditioned for the role of Cho Chang on a whim. Her father suggested she stop by and try out before she went shopping.

116. JK Rowling initially insisted that the entire cast (including the director) be British, but eventually relented on both requests.

117. The actor who played Dudley Dursley lost so much weight between the second and third movie that the production team almost had to recast him. Eventually they made it work with a fat suit.

118. Dumbledore was in love with Gellert Grindelwald.

119. In the movies, Dolores Umbridge is the only character whose color theme is pink. Even Tonk's hair is left purple.

120. In the fifth movie, in the scene where Harry, Ron, and Hermione are discussing Harry's kissing Cho, the three begin to crack up near the end of the scene. This was real laughter from the actors. The director thought it was great for the scene and kept rolling.

121. In *Deathly Hallows Part 1,* Dobby tells Ron how good it is to see him again, but they had never met in the movies.

122. The Harry Potter books are one of Stephen King's favorite series.

123. The actor who played Ron (Rupert Grint) used some of the money he made from the Harry Potter movies to start an ice-cream business. He also bought his brother James a race-car and helped him become a serious competitor in the UK circuit.

124. Daniel Radcliffe can't wear contact lenses, so in the scenes where Harry is possessed, his eyes have been digitally changed.

125. Dolores Umbridge was based on a co-worker at the school JK Rowling taught at. They hated each other though JK Rowling was never sure why. Just one of those things.

126. Robert Pattinson enjoyed his role as Cedric Diggory much more than Edward Cullen from the Twilight series.

127. In the movies, the stonework of Hogwarts is almost 100% plaster. The plaster was painted over and aged to appear as if made of stone and hundreds of years old.

128. Warner Brothers received more than 100 death threats for pushing the release date of *Half-Blood Prince* to 2009 when it was scheduled to be released in fall 2008.

129. Drew Barrymore had a cameo written into the first movie but the scene was later cut.

130. There are 700 different fouls in Quidditch.

131. *Chamber of Secrets* and *Order of the Phoenix* are the only two Harry Potter films *not* to be nominated for an academy award.

132. Voldemort is half-blooded despite having a hatred for half-bloods.

133. Over the course of the films, Harry's lightning bolt scar was applied by make-up specialists more than 5,000 times. It holds the record for the smallest/most expensive make-up in film history.

134. Most of the Hermione torture scene from *Deathly Hallows* had to be cut from the final version because otherwise the movie would have gotten an R rating.

135. For the fifth movie, JK Rowling provided over 70 names for the Black family tree tapestry. She also indicated which names were to be scorched.

136. Dedalus Diggle was wearing purple robes when he first met Harry.

137. Harry Potter's favorite food is Treacle Tart.

138. Madam Hooch was completely written out of all Harry Potter movies because the actress wanted too much money to portray her.

139. Caio Cesar, a Brazilian voice actor who dubbed Daniel Radcliffe as Harry Potter, was also a police officer and died when he was only 27 after being shot in his neck in the slums of Rio de Janeiro.

140. In the films, the thick books in Dumbledore's library are phone books that have been doctored up by the art department.

141. Daniel Radcliffe broke more than 100 prop wands because he was using them off-screen as drumsticks. His "drums" were plastic coffee containers.

142. There is no wizard university so all "professor" titles are honorary. JK Rowling has alluded that teachers must apprentice under other wizards to obtain a teaching position.

143. In order to get acquainted with the three lead actors, director Alfonso Cuarón had each one of them write an essay about their characters. Emma Watson wrote a 16-page essay. Daniel Radcliffe wrote a one-page summary. Rupert Grint never even bothered to turned his in.

144. To prevent pirates from recording illegal copies of *Prisoner of Azkaban* Warner Brothers issued night vision goggles to movie theaters.

145. Dobby's last words are the same as the first words he says to Harry Potter.

146. Nigel Wolpert only appears in the Harry Potter movies. He does not appear at all in the books. But the screenwriters have said he combines aspects of Colin Creevey and Dennis Creevey.

147. Robbie Coltrane turned down a great part in *The West Wing* to reprise his role as Hagrid.

148. In the first movie, Crabbe and Goyle have no lines of dialogue.

149. Terry Gilliam (JK Rowling's first choice director for the first movie) was offered the chance to direct the sixth movie, but he was still angry at not being offered *Sorcerer's Stone* that he said no.

150. In the fifth movie, Harry's scream in the Department of Mysteries was digitally altered because focus groups found it was too disturbing to listen to.

151. Oliver Wood played for the Puddlemere United Quidditch team.

152. The color palette and lighting methods used in *Harry Potter and the Half-Blood Prince* were heavily influenced by Rembrant.

153. In the last movie, Voldemort hugging Draco wasn't in the script, but rather improvised by Ralph Fiennes. Tom Felton's blank stare and confused reaction wasn't acting.

154. The Battle of Hogwarts was fought on May 2nd, 1998.